Classic Nursery Tales

Classic Nursery Tales

Retold and illustrated
by Graham Percy

PAVILION
CHILDREN'S

For little Merle – Gr

This edition first published in the United Kingdom in 2010
by Pavilion Children's Books
an imprint of Anova Books Group Ltd
10 Southcombe Street
London W14 0RA

Design copyright © Pavilion Children's Books
Text and illustration copyright © Graham Percy

A CIP catalogue record for this book is available from
the British Library.

ISBN 9781843651529

Repro by Mission Productions Ltd. Hong Kong.
Printed by Craft Print

CONTENTS

THE THREE LITTLE PIGS   6

THE PORRIDGE POT   13

HENNY-PENNY   19

THE GINGERBREAD MAN   26

THE HARE AND THE TORTOISE   32

THE KING AND THE MOON   38

THE TURNIP   44

THE COUNTRY MOUSE AND THE TOWN MOUSE   51

GOLDILOCKS AND THE THREE BEARS   58

MR FOX'S BAG   66

THE MUSICIANS OF BREMEN   74

THE UGLY DUCKLING   83

HOW THE NIGHT SKY BECAME BRIGHTER   90

THE THREE LITTLE PIGS

Once upon a time there were three little pigs. Early one morning the little pigs decided to leave home and go out into the big, wide world to seek their fortune. Their mother gave them a bundle of food and some money.

'Now make me one promise,' said their mother. 'You must each build a little house where you can be safe and warm. There may be a hungry wolf out there, looking for little pigs — so do be careful!'

She gave them a big hug and an even bigger kiss – and off they went, trot, trot, trot down the road.

When they reached the crossroads they went in different directions.

The first little pig went up the hill to the farm. The second little pig went down the hill to the forest. And the third little pig walked all the way to the sea.

When the first little pig got to the farm he met a farmer beside the front gate piling up straw.

'That would be a quick way to make a house,' thought the little pig. So he asked if he could buy some straw.

'Of course,' said the farmer. 'Here is straw for your walls and straw for your roof.' Soon the little pig had built a house made of straw.

Just before sunset along came the wolf. He knocked at the door.

'Little pig, little pig, let me come in,' he said. 'No, no, no, not by the hairs on my chinny, chin, chin, I won't let you come in,' said the little pig. 'Then I'll huff and I'll puff and I'll blow your house down,' said the wolf.

And he huffed and he puffed and he blew the house down and ate up the little pig.

When the second little pig reached the forest he saw a forester piling up sticks.

He asked the man for a big bundle of sticks. 'Certainly,' said the man.

'Here are sticks for your walls and sticks for your roof.'

In no time at all the second little pig had built a house of sticks.

But sooner rather than later, along came the wolf.

He knocked at the door.
'Little pig, little pig, let me
come in.'

'No, no, no, not
by the hairs on my
chinny, chin, chin,
I won't let you come in,'
said the little pig.

'Then I'll huff and I'll puff
and I'll blow your house down,'
growled the wolf. And he huffed and he
puffed and he blew the house down and ate up the
second little pig.

Now the third little pig had almost reached the
sea when he met a man making bricks.

'I'd like to buy a pile of bricks,' said the little pig.

'Right,' said the man, 'here are bricks for your
walls and tiles for your roof.'

Very soon the little pig had built a house made of
bricks. It had a wonderful view of the sea.

But sooner rather than later, along came the wolf, knocking at the door.

'Little pig, little pig, let me come in.'

'No, no, no, not by the hairs on my chinny, chin, chin, I won't let you come in,' said the little pig.

'Then I'll huff and I'll puff and I'll blow your house down,' snarled the wolf.

And he huffed and he puffed, and he puffed and he huffed, but he could not blow down the little pig's house made of bricks.

Then the wolf grew very angry.

He shouted down the chimney, 'Little pig, I'm coming down the chimney to catch you and then I'll eat you up for my dinner.'

'OH NO YOU WON'T!' shouted the little pig. He was ready for the wolf. He put a big pot of water on the fire. Soon the water was boiling hot.

'I'm coming to get you,' shouted the wolf as he climbed down the chimney.

CRASH! He fell straight into the pot of boiling water with a SPLASH!

The little pig slammed the lid on the pot and that was the end of the wicked old wolf.

And the little pig lived happily in his little brick house for the rest of his life. Sometimes his mother came to visit. They would sit down together and enjoy the view out to sea.

THE PORRIDGE POT

Once upon a time there was a little girl who lived with her mother in a little house at the edge of a little village. They were very poor and had no money to buy food. Every day the little girl went into the forest to collect berries for them to eat.

One day while she was walking in the forest she saw an old woman carrying a big bundle on her back. The old woman said in a croaky voice, 'You look hungry my dear.'

'Yes I am,' replied the little girl. 'My mother and I have no money for food. See how thin my tummy has grown.'

The old woman smiled kindly and opened her bundle. There stood a fat black cooking pot.

'This will help you my dear. Whenever you and your mother are hungry just say, "Cook, little pot, cook." As soon as you say these words, and these words alone, then the pot will begin to steam and bubble. Soon it will fill up with hot porridge.

'When you've had enough just say, "Stop, little pot, stop." Then the pot will stop making porridge. Now remember the words, for no others will do.'

The little girl was thrilled. She said to the old woman, 'Oh, thank you, thank you.'

Then she took the pot home to her mother and they put it on the kitchen table.

'Cook, little pot, cook,' said the little girl. They peered into the pot. It began to steam and bubble. Soon it had filled with hot porridge.

'Stop, little pot, stop,' said the little girl and the pot stopped making porridge.

The little girl and her mother hugged one another and danced for joy. They knew that they would never be hungry again. Then they sat down and ate so much that their tummies were as tight as a drum.

Now, one day the little girl went to visit her grandmother in another village. While she was gone her mother began to feel hungry. So she got out the fat black pot and put it on the kitchen table. 'Cook little pot, cook,' she said. Sure enough the pot steamed and bubbled and filled with hot porridge.

When the pot was full, the little girl's mother said, 'Enough, pot, enough.'

But the pot went on making hot porridge. There was so much porridge that it came out of the pot and over the table and on to the floor.

'Oh dear,' cried the little girl's mother, 'I can't remember how to stop the pot making porridge.'

She tried again, calling out, 'No, pot, stop.'

But of course, it was no good. She had forgotten the magic words.

By now the porridge was pouring out through the window. It poured into the yard outside and then into the house next door. It ran down the street and made its way through shop doorways. It ran into the fields and on to the playground.

It crept up stairs and flooded the market place.

Soon there was porridge, porridge everywhere. Before long the whole village was filled with porridge.

The villagers were so afraid that they ran away, in case the huge sea of porridge swallowed them up.

Just then the little girl came home. 'Stop, little pot, stop,' she said calmly. The fat black pot stopped making porridge.

The little girl's mother decided that she would have to learn the right words to say, or they would need to buy a porridge boat!

And as for the villagers; they had to eat their way through all the porridge in the streets and the yards, so that they could get back into their houses.

Well, after that nobody felt hungry again for a very long time!

HENNY-PENNY

One day Henny-Penny was peck, peck, pecking at some corn in the farmyard when – whack! – an acorn fell and hit her – smack! – on the head!

'Goodness me!' said Henny-Penny. 'The sky is falling on my head. I must go and tell the king.'

So off she rushed... But on the way she met Cocky-Locky.

I'm going to tell the king that the sky is falling on my head,' said Henny-Penny.

'May I come too?' asked Cocky-Locky.

'Of course you can,' replied Henny-Penny and off they rushed together.

So they walked and they walked until they met Ducky-Daddies.

'We're going to tell the king that the sky is falling down,' said Henny-Penny and Cocky-Locky.

'May I come too?' asked Ducky-Daddies.

'Of course you can,' replied Henny-Penny and Cocky-Locky, and off they rushed together.

They walked and they walked until they met Goosey-Poosey.

'We're going to tell the king that the sky is falling down,' said Henny-Penny, Cocky-Locky and Ducky-Daddies.

'May I come too?' asked Goosey-Poosey.

'Of course you can,' replied Henny-Penny, Cocky-Locky and Ducky-Daddies and off they rushed together.

They walked and they walked until they met Turkey-Lurkey.

'We're going to tell the king that the sky is falling down,' said Henny-Penny, Cocky-Locky, Ducky-Daddies and Goosey-Poosey.

'May I come too?' asked Turkey-Lurkey.

'Of course you can,' replied Henny-Penny, Cocky-Locky, Ducky-Daddies and Goosey-Poosey.

They walked and they walked until they met Foxy-Woxy.

'We're going to tell the king that the sky is falling down,' said Henny-Penny, Cocky-Locky, Ducky-Daddies, Goosey-Poosey and Turkey-Lurkey.

'May I come too?' asked Foxy-Woxy.

'Of course you can,' replied Henny-Penny, Cocky-Locky, Ducky-Daddies, Goosey-Poosey and Turkey-Lurkey, and off they rushed together.

Now Foxy-Woxy was as thin as a whistle and hungry as the wind, so he called out to the others, 'Follow me, dear friends, for I know the quickest way to the king's palace.'

So they followed Foxy-Woxy, and he led them to a dark, narrow hole between some tree roots.

Now this was the door to Foxy-Woxy's den, but the others did not know this.

Foxy-Woxy turned to them all and said, 'This is the short-cut to the king's palace. I'll go in first and you follow me, one at a time.'

So Foxy-Woxy slipped into his den. He stopped a little way in and waited. No sooner had he disappeared into the dark, narrow hole than in went Turkey-Lurkey.

Down the hole ran Turkey-Lurkey to where Foxy-Woxy lay waiting.

Foxy-Woxy opened his jaws and there was a SNAP, and a hrumph! and poor Turkey-Lurkey was gone! Foxy-Woxy had eaten her!

Down the hole ran Goosey-Poosey.

And there was a SNAP and a hrumph! and poor Goosey-Poosey was gone. Foxy-Woxy had eaten her!

Down the hole ran Ducky-Daddies.

And there was a SNAP and a hrumph! and poor Ducky-Daddies was gone. Foxy-Woxy had eaten him!

Down the hole ran Cocky-Locky. But he heard all the snapping and hrumphing, so he called out to Henny-Penny,

'Henny-Penny, Henny-Penny, don't come in!'

So Henny-Penny turned tail and ran away home, with the hungry wind rushing along behind her. So it was that she never did tell the king that the sky was falling on her head.

THE GINGERBREAD MAN

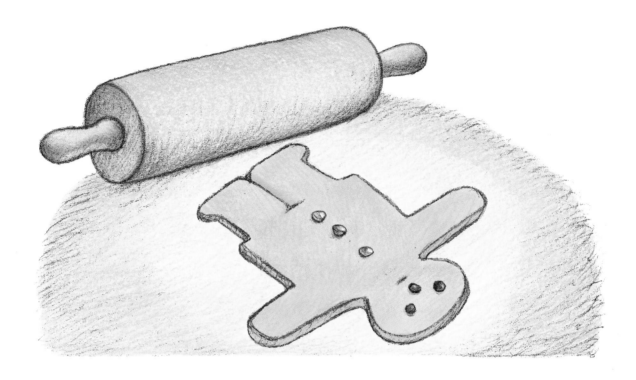

There was once an old woman who thought she would make something nice for her husband's birthday. So she rolled out some gingerbread and made the shape of a little man. She put raisins for his eyes, a raisin for his nose and bits of ginger for coat buttons. Then she popped him in the oven.

When she opened the oven door she had such a surprise! The little gingerbread man leapt out and ran across the kitchen to the door.

He stopped at the door and called back to the little old woman,

'Run, run as fast as you can,

You can't catch me,

I'm the gingerbread man!'

Then he ran through the garden, straight past where the old man was working, and off down the lane.

'Stop, stop!' shouted the old man and the old woman, but they could not catch him.

The little gingerbread man ran on until he came to a cow in a field by the lane.

'Yum, yum,' said the cow. 'You look good enough to eat.' But the little gingerbread man raced on down the lane calling back to the cow, 'Run, run as fast as you can, You can't catch me, I'm the

gingerbread man!' And the cow could not catch him.

Then the gingerbread man came to a stream where there was an old horse drinking. The horse looked at the little gingerbread man and said, 'Mmm, you look good enough to eat!'

But the gingerbread man darted past the old horse and called back to him, 'Run, run as fast as you can, You can't catch me, I'm the gingerbread man.' And the horse could not catch him.

The little gingerbread man ran on along the river bank. Suddenly a fox sprang out from behind a bush. There was no way past the fox for the little gingerbread man and he could not cross the stream. The fox gave a cunning grin. He bent down and said, 'I'll help you across the stream. Sit

on my bushy tail and I will swim you over to the other side.'

So the gingerbread man climbed on to the fox's tail. The fox leaped into the stream and began to swim. He thought to himself, 'This little fellow is going to make a very nice snack for me!'

Then the fox said to the little gingerbread man, 'Maybe you are getting a bit wet sitting on my tail. Why don't you jump on to my back?' So the little gingerbread man jumped on to his back.

Then the fox said to the little gingerbread man, 'You make it hard for me to swim, sitting on my back.

Why don't you jump on to my

nose?' So the little gingerbread man jumped on to his nose.

And, just as they reached the bank on the other side SNAP! went the fox's sharp teeth.

'Oh dear me,' said the little gingerbread man, 'I'm half gone.'

Then SNAP! again went the fox's teeth.

'Oh dear me,' said the little gingerbread man, 'I'm three-quarters gone.'

Then SNAP! went the fox again and this time I'm afraid there was nothing left at all of that little gingerbread man.

THE HARE AND THE TORTOISE

There was once a hare who was always showing off to the other animals.

'I'm the fastest creature in the whole wide world,' he boasted to them all. 'And you,' he sneered at an old tortoise who was lying quietly under a bush, enjoying the sun, 'you must be the slowest creature in the whole wide world.'

The tortoise looked up thoughtfully and replied: 'Why don't we have a race to see if you are right?'

The hare just rolled on the ground laughing.

'You must be crazy to think that you can beat me in a race,' he sneered. So the hare and the tortoise walked over to a nearby tree stump.

'This will be the start,' said the hare. 'We'll race up to the end of the lake and the first one back to this tree stump will be the winner.'

All the other animals were very excited and quickly gathered round. They asked a little field mouse to be the referee. The mouse jumped up on to the tree stump. He waved a twig and squeaked, 'Ready! Steady! Go!' The hare shot off, leaping ahead with his long, strong legs. The old tortoise plodded along behind in his slow and steady way. Soon the hare was far in front of him.

When the hare reached the end of the lake, he was quite out of breath. I'm feeling a bit puffed, he thought to himself, but as tortoise is so slow, and so far behind, I have plenty of time for a rest.

So he lay down in the long grass. And soon he was fast asleep.

Some time after this the old tortoise plodded up to where the hare lay sleeping. When the hare started to snore, the tortoise just smiled to himself and kept plodding along – slow and steady, slow and steady, slow and steady...

34

The hare didn't wake up until the sun was going down.

'Oh no!' he cried, 'I must have overslept. I had better rush off and finish this ridiculous race.'

Meanwhile, the old tortoise had nearly reached the tree trunk. He was getting nearer and nearer to the end of the race.

Along came the hare, rushing like the wind, looking quite angry.

But the tortoise beat the boastful hare to the tree trunk. All the other animals leapt in the air, yelping and squealing for joy.

The hare slumped to the ground. He looked very hot and bothered and, yes, quite angry!

Well done, Mr Tortoise,' squeaked the little field mouse. 'You are the winner. Slow and steady won the race for you.'

And all the other animals clapped and cheered and chanted, 'Slow and steady won the race, slow and steady won the race!'

THE KING AND THE MOON

There was once a king who had everything. He had a thousand cattle, he had peacocks in his garden, he had plates made of gold and shoes made of silver. But he still wanted more. More than anything else he wanted to touch the moon.

Late one night as he was gazing upwards an idea came to him. The moon looked so close. Why not build a tower to climb up to it?

So the next day he called all the carpenters in the land to his palace and announced his plan.

'Not up to the sky?' they all cried.

'Yes, up to the sky and if you don't make the tower for me, I'll chop off your heads!' the king growled back at them.

So the king's soldiers and carpenters travelled through the land searching for wood. They thought and thought about how they could build a tower that would reach up to the sky.

'We will make boxes and pile them them up, one on top of another. The king can climb to the top, and try to reach the moon...'

Day after day they worked, until they had cut down every tree in the land. Then the carpenters made a thousand and one boxes. The soldiers piled them all up, one on top of another.

The top of the pile was hidden in the clouds.

'Your majesty,' said one soldier. 'The tower looks rather wobbly. Let me climb it first in case it is dangerous and falls down.'

'Never!' shouted the king. 'I'm not letting a soldier climb to the moon before I do. I'll do the climbing, thank you very much!'

Everyone in the kingdom came to see the king climb the tower of boxes. It was very, very high. It reached way above the clouds. It was also very, very shaky.

The king started to climb. Up and up he went, till all that the people below could see was the odd flash of gold from his crown.

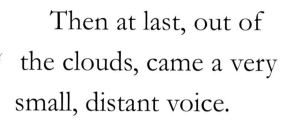

Then at last, out of
the clouds, came a very
small, distant voice.

'I'm almost there,' he
was shouting. 'I just need one
more box!'

'There are none left,' shouted
back the soldiers.

'None left!' roared the king.
'Then pull out one of the boxes
from the bottom and send it up
to me.'

'Are you sure?' shouted
the soldiers.

Now, even the children
could see what would happen if
the soldiers did as he asked.

But everyone was afraid
to disobey the king's
orders.

They were afraid he might chop off their heads.
So they set to and pulled out a box from the bottom of the pile.

First there was a-creaking and a-groaning and
then a-splintering, a-smashing and a-crashing.
Down came the tower. The king fell, spinning
down from the clouds. He came down much faster
than he went up. Soon he landed and he found
that he was seeing stars!

I'll tell you this as well – it cured the king of
wanting to touch the moon.

THE TURNIP

There was once an old man with a garden full of vegetables. He grew vegetables all the year round: cabbages, cucumbers, carrots and kale. The old man and his wife always had plenty to eat. They even had enough for the children next door.

One spring morning the old man was planting a row of turnip seeds. He raked the soil over the line of seeds and whispered to them.

'Now grow, grow, my little ones.'

And he bent down and whispered to the last little seed, 'And you especially.'

Sooner rather than later the green shoots came up through the soil. In no time there were bunches of leaves. The turnips grew bigger and bigger. At the end of the row was the biggest of them all.

The old man's wife thought to herself, 'That turnip would make a wonderful soup.' So she said to her husband, 'Why don't you pull up that enormous turnip, so we can have turnip soup for supper?'

So the old man grabbed the enormous turnip. He pulled as hard as he could. But the turnip would not budge. No, not one bit.

So he called his wife. And the old woman pulled the old man, and the old man pulled the turnip. But the turnip would not budge at all. No, not one bit.

So the old woman went next door to fetch the little boy and the little girl. And they pulled the old woman, and she pulled the old man, and the old man pulled the turnip. But still the turnip would not budge at all. No, not one bit.

The little boy and the little girl saw a young fox watching. They called to him to come and help.

So the fox pulled the little boy and the little girl, and they pulled the old woman, and she pulled the old man. And he pulled the turnip. But still the turnip would not budge at all. No, not one bit.

So the fox beckoned to the old folks' cat to come and help them.

And the cat pulled the fox, and the fox pulled

the little boy and the little girl, and they pulled the old woman, and she pulled the old man. And he pulled the turnip and... still the turnip would not budge. No, not one bit.

Then the cat saw her old playmate the grey mouse and she mewed for him to come and help. So the mouse pulled the cat, and the cat

pulled the fox, and the fox pulled the children, and the children pulled the old woman, and the old woman pulled the old man. And he pulled the turnip, till suddenly...

There was a crick, and a crack, and the ground gave way, and they all fell back as out popped the most enormous turnip... at last!

That night they were so tired that they fell asleep by the giant turnip.

The next day the old woman made it into the most delicious turnip soup they had ever eaten. And there was enough for them all to come back for some more every day for the rest of the week.

THE COUNTRY MOUSE
AND THE TOWN MOUSE

Once upon a time there was a country mouse who lived under a hedge in the countryside. Every morning he swept out his house. Then he went out into the fields and woods to collect seeds, nuts and berries to eat. Every night when he snuggled into his warm bed he thought to himself, 'What a lucky country mouse I am.'

One day a town mouse came to stay.

He was the country mouse's cousin. The country mouse made a delicious supper of berries, nuts and apples. He even gave up his own soft, mossy bed for his cousin to sleep in.

Soon the town mouse was fast asleep, while the country mouse lay awake tossing and turning. 'I wonder whether my cousin is comfortable,' he thought to himself. 'I wonder whether he enjoyed his supper.'

Later that night, when he was still awake, he imagined what a grand town house his cousin must live in and what a fabulous feather bed he must sleep in.

The next day, when they were walking through the nearby cornfield looking for more seeds and berries, the town mouse suddenly stopped.

There in front of them was a huge creature about to rush at the pair of them. 'Quick,'

squealed the country mouse, 'it's a weasel!' He tugged his cousin to safety under some brambles. They sat under the brambles and brushed themselves down.

The town mouse hissed angrily, 'I've had enough of this countryside of yours. I've been scratched by brambles and frightened by a creature I've never seen before. I have had to sleep on a pile of rubbish and eat the meanest of meals too! I am going back to town. Why don't you join me?'

The country mouse was thrilled. He quickly made a bundle of things to take with him and they set off.

It was dark when they arrived in the town and the country mouse was dazzled by the lights.

As well as the strange bright lights there was the thumping and banging of people's feet as they walked along the hard stone pavements.

Soon the mice stopped in front of a magnificent house. It was just as big and as grand as the country mouse had imagined!

In they went through a hole in the wall and came out in a grand dining room. The town mouse beckoned to the country mouse to join him on the table. There the country mouse could hardly believe his eyes. Plates and bowls and dishes were filled with nuts and cheese and biscuits and even piles of strawberries and cherries.

'Take your pick,' said the town mouse grandly, as he started nibbling away at the wonderful feast spread before them on the table.

'Try this cake,' squeaked the country mouse, turning to the town mouse. But the town mouse had disappeared and, what was worse, on the other side of the table were two ears, two eyes, then the huge face of the household cat.

The country mouse was terrified. Then he felt a frantic tug on his tail. 'Over here, quick!' came a whisper from behind a large silver coffee pot. It was the town mouse. They leapt to the floor and raced to the hole in the wall.

In the dark passage inside the wall the town mouse tugged at his country cousin.

'Up this way to my magnificent feather bed.' There they lay down to sleep. But the country mouse could not sleep at all and lay trembling. The town mouse snored away next to him.

In the morning the country mouse had his things ready.

'Cousin, I am going home right now.'

'Oh no, let's go and see the town,' replied the town mouse. But the country mouse was off: back to his cosy house under the hedge, far away in the countryside.

And when he reached home, he never thought again about grand town houses and magnificent dinner tables and feather beds. He was very happy indeed to be a country mouse, with his seeds and nuts and berries from the wood and his soft little mossy bed.

GOLDILOCKS AND THE THREE BEARS

Once upon a time there were three bears who lived in a house deep in the woods. There was Father Bear and Mother Bear and Baby Bear.

In the kitchen they each had a bowl for their porridge. There was a great big bowl for Father Bear, a medium-sized bowl for Mother Bear and a teeny-weeny bowl for Baby Bear.

In the living room they each had a chair to sit on. There was a great big chair for Father Bear, a medium-sized chair for Mother Bear and a teeny-weeny chair for Baby Bear.

Upstairs they each had a bed to sleep in: a great big bed for Father Bear, a medium-sized bed for Mother Bear and a teeny-weeny bed for Baby Bear.

One morning, Mother Bear made some porridge for their breakfast. She poured it into the three bowls. But it was too hot to eat right away, so the three bears went for a walk in the woods while the porridge cooled.

While they were out, a little girl called Goldilocks came walking by. When she saw the house she went up to the front door.

She knocked at the door but no one came, so she gently turned the door handle and peeped in.

'What a cosy house,' said Goldilocks to herself. 'I wonder who lives here?' She tiptoed inside, closing the door quietly behind her.

First she went into the kitchen. She saw the three bowls of porridge on the table. She was feeling quite hungry so she thought, 'I'll have just one taste.'

First she took a spoonful from the great big bowl, but that was too hot.

Then she took a spoonful from the medium-sized bowl, but that was too cold. Then she took a spoonful from the teeny-weeny bowl and that was just right. So she ate it all up!

Goldilocks felt so full of porridge that she wanted to sit down.

First she sat in the great big chair, but that was too hard.

Then she sat in the medium-sized chair, but that was too soft.

Then she sat on the teeny-weeny chair, but when she did – CRACK! – the little chair broke into pieces and Goldilocks ended up on the floor!

'Oh dear,' said Goldilocks, 'I think I'd better go upstairs and lie down.'

First, she lay down on the great big bed, but that was too hard.

Then she lay down on the medium-sized bed, but that was too soft.

Then she lay down on the teeny-weeny bed and that was just right. Goldilocks fell fast asleep.

While she was sleeping the three bears came back from their walk in the woods.

They were all very hungry after their walk in the woods, so they went straight to their bowls of porridge.

'Somebody's been eating my porridge!' roared Father Bear in his big gruff voice.

'Somebody's been eating my porridge!' said Mother Bear in her soft gentle voice.

'Somebody's been eating my porridge and they've eaten it all up!' squeaked Baby Bear in his teeny-weeny voice.

The bears ran into the living room.

'Somebody's been sitting in my chair!' growled Father Bear in his big gruff voice. 'Somebody's been sitting in my chair!' said Mother Bear in her sweet soft voice.

'Somebody's been sitting in my chair and they've broken it!' squeaked Baby Bear in his teeny-weeny voice.

'QUICK!' roared Father Bear, 'Let's look upstairs!' The bears ran up to the bedroom.

'Somebody's been sleeping in my bed!' growled Father Bear in his great big voice. 'Somebody's been sleeping in my bed!' said Mother Bear in her soft voice.

'Somebody's been sleeping in my bed – and she's still there!' squeaked Baby Bear in his teeny-weeny voice.

At that moment Goldilocks woke up. When she saw the three bears she jumped out of the teeny-weeny bed, ran down the stairs, out of the house, into the woods and all the way home.

Then Mother Bear made some more porridge, while Father Bear mended the little chair and Baby Bear looked sadly out of the window. He wished and wished that the little girl had stayed to play with him.

Mr Fox's Bag

Early one morning Mr Fox was woken up by a loud buzzzzz. He had been fast asleep under an old apple tree. There was a fat bumble-bee right on top of his nose.

'Groink,' he snorted, and he popped the fat bumble-bee into his bag.

Then Mr Fox walked down the road till he came to a house. There was a woman dressed in blue, sweeping the path.

'Good morning,' said Mr Fox.

'May I leave my bag here? I'm just going next door.'

'Of course you can,' said the woman dressed in blue.

'Thank you,' said Mr Fox. 'But mind you don't look in my bag.' And off he went.

Well, I'm afraid the woman did peep in the bag. As soon as she opened it, out flew the bumble-bee into the farmyard. The little woman's cockerel ran after the bumble-bee and gobbled him up!

When Mr Fox came back, the woman said, 'I'm sorry, but I'm afraid I peeped into your bag and the fat bumble-bee flew out and my cockerel gobbled him up.'

'Oh, really!' said Mr Fox. 'Then I shall take your cockerel and put him into my bag instead.'

So off went Mr Fox and he walked and walked along the streets until he came to another house where there was a woman dressed in green, sitting outside in the sun, knitting.

'Good morning,' said Mr Fox. 'May I leave my bag here? I'm just going next door.'

'Of course you can,' said the woman dressed in green.

'Thank you,' said Mr Fox.

'But mind you don't look in my bag.' And off he went.

Well, I'm afraid that the woman did peep in the bag. As soon as she opened the bag, out flew the cockerel. The woman's pet pig chased him round the garden and out into the fields.

When Mr Fox came back, the woman apologised to him saying, 'I'm so sorry, but I looked in your bag and out flew the cockerel and I'm afraid my pet pig chased him into the fields.'

'Oh really!' said Mr Fox. 'Then I shall take your pet pig and put him in my bag instead.'

So off went Mr Fox and he walked and walked along the streets until he came to a house where a woman dressed in red was making gingerbread men on a table.

69

'Good morning,' said Mr Fox. 'May I leave my bag here? I'm just going next door.'

'Of course you can,' said the woman dressed in red.

'Thank you,' said Mr Fox. 'But mind you don't look in my bag.' And off he went.

Sitting beside the woman was a big dog. He was waiting to be given a gingerbread man to eat.

'Ssh!' exclaimed the woman to her hungry dog as she gingerly opened the bag to have a peep.

'Oink, oink,' went the pig as he leapt out of the bag and ran away home.

'Oh dear,' thought the woman dressed in red. 'What will Mr Fox do when he finds nothing in his bag?'

So she put her big dog into the bag and waited. When Mr Fox returned he looked at the bag.

Mr Fox thought, 'Well the pet pig is still in there.'

And he gave the bag a poke with a stick just to make sure.

Well, the dog did not like being poked with a stick and he leapt out of the bag, barking angrily.

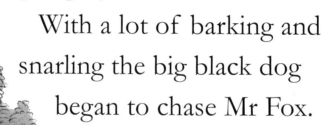

With a lot of barking and snarling the big black dog began to chase Mr Fox. He chased him all the way out of the town and right over the hills till he could not be seen any more.

But the dog soon came bouncing back to the woman dressed in red and the table with all those gingerbread men.

And as a special reward the woman gave him not just one gingerbread man, but as many as he could eat, because he was so hungry, and because he had chased away Mr Fox.

THE MUSICIANS OF BREMEN

There was once a donkey who worked hard all day. Every day he carried heavy sacks of corn to the mill. One day the donkey's master said to him, 'You're getting too old and slow to be any use to me. You'll just have to go.'

Of course the donkey was very unhappy, but then he thought, 'I can still bray beautifully. All the other donkeys say what a fine voice I have. I shall go to Bremen and sing with the town band.'

So off he went, trot-trotting down the road to Bremen. Soon he met a dog lying beside the road. The dog looked very unhappy. 'My master has thrown me out,' said the dog. 'He says I'm too old to round-up sheep any more.'

'But surely you can still bark?' asked the donkey.

'Yes, of course,' replied the dog.

'Then come with me and we'll join the town band. You can bark and I can bray.' So off they went together — the donkey trot-trotting and the dog pat-pattering down the road towards Bremen.

Before long they came across a cat sitting on a wall. The cat looked very unhappy.

'My mistress says I have to go because I'm too old to catch mice,' miaowed the cat.

Why not come with us to Bremen?' said the donkey. 'We're going to join the band there. I can bray, the dog can bark and you can miaow.'

'I'd like that,' said the cat. So off they went together – the donkey trot-trotting, the dog pat-pattering and the cat pad-padding down the road towards Bremen.

They'd not gone far when they came to a cockerel sitting on a gatepost. He was crowing very loudly, but not looking at all happy.

What's the matter?' asked the donkey.

'The farmer's wife says I'm too old to be useful any more,' said the cockerel. 'So I'm making as much noise as I possibly can before she puts me into the cooking pot.'

'Well, why not come with us to Bremen?' asked the donkey. We're going to join the town band there. I can bray, the dog can bark, the cat can miaow and you can crow.'

The cockerel was delighted, so off they went together – the donkey trot-trotting, the dog pat-pattering, the cat pad-padding and the cockerel scritch-scratching down the road towards Bremen.

Then it began to get dark, so the animals went up to a farmhouse beside the road to Bremen.

'Maybe we can ask here for something to eat and a place to sleep,' suggested the donkey to the other animals.

He looked through the kitchen window and what do you think he saw? A bunch of wild-looking robbers. They were devouring a feast of food at the kitchen table.

Now the donkey and his friends were very hungry. How could they trick these wild-looking robbers?

The donkey had a plan. He put his hoofs up on the window sill and the dog scrambled up on his back. Then the cat climbed on to the dog's shoulders and the cockerel perched on the cat's head. Then together they all started to sing at the tops of their voices.

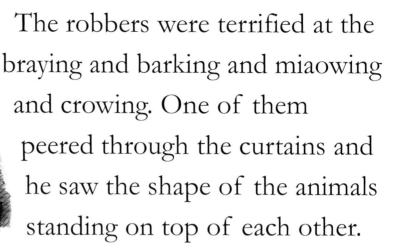

The robbers were terrified at the braying and barking and miaowing and crowing. One of them peered through the curtains and he saw the shape of the animals standing on top of each other.

'It's a giant roaring,' he screamed. The robbers were so frightened that they ran out of the house and into the woods, with their teeth chattering and their legs knocking with fear.

So the four friends went inside and enjoyed a hearty meal before putting out the candles and lying down to sleep.

While they were sleeping the wildest robber crept back into the house.

He had come back to find the bag of gold they had left behind.

He tiptoed into the kitchen but, in the darkness, he trod on the cat's tail. The cat hissed and spat and scratched his arm.

'Yeeow!' cried the robber. He stumbled back to the door, but he tripped over the dog, who leapt up and bit him on the leg.

'Ouch!' cried the robber as he staggered away from the dog... bumping into the donkey, who kicked him straight through the kitchen door.

As he landed, the cockerel flapped his wings in his face and screeched in his ears.

That was enough for the wildest robber. He rushed off into the woods to tell the others.

'In the kitchen there was a snake that hissed, and a wolf that bit me, and a giant that threw me outside where a hobgoblin flew in my face!'

The robbers ran off and were never seen again.

Meanwhile the donkey, the dog, the cat and the cockerel had become such good friends that they decided to live together in the farmhouse.

And so it was that they never did go and sing with the Bremen town band!

THE UGLY DUCKLING

Once upon a time there was a mother duck with nine little ducklings. Now eight of the ducklings were pretty, fluffy things, but the ninth duckling was not. He was rather an ugly duckling. He was dirty grey with a long neck.

'What an ugly little duckling you are!' his mother said to him. His brothers and sisters teased him and pecked him. Then they tried to chase him away.

We don't want to play with you. We are pretty but you are ugly!' they said.

So when the whole family went for a walk around the banks of the pond the ugly duckling stayed well behind, away from his brothers and sisters. And when their mother taught the others to swim and dive under the water, he did not join them but just looked on. He was very unhappy.

One day they all went to another pond nearby and, as usual, the ugly duckling lagged well behind the others. When the ducks in the other pond saw him they cackled with laughter.

What on earth is this ugly thing?' said one of them.

'You can't possibly be a duck!' shrieked another, and she gave him a sharp peck.

'I am a duck! I am!' cried the ugly duckling and he ran away into some reeds where they wouldn't find him.

Soon it was night and the ugly duckling wondered where his mother was. He tried to find his way home, but he was well and truly lost. He felt lonely without his brothers and sisters. Even though they made fun of him, they were the only family he had.

The next morning the ugly duckling was quite alone. He was looking for food in the water when two wild ducks splashed down nearby.

'What kind of bird are you?' one of them asked.

'I'm a duck,' said the ugly duckling quietly.

Funny kind of duck!' the ducks chuckled to one another as they flew off.

Then the ugly duckling set off across the fields until he came to another pond. There were more reeds to hide in and plenty of food in the water so he stayed there all through the winter.

One day when it was very cold and the wind was blowing he saw some swans flying overhead. They were so graceful with their great, white wings beating slowly through the sky.

'We're going south,' they called down to him. 'Why don't you come with us?'

'Yes I will,' cried the ugly duckling, eager to join the swans, for he had had no-one to know and nowhere to go. But when he flapped his little grey wings he could not take off.

Why, he could hardly fly at all. So he just watched the big, beautiful swans until they were far away.

The winter dragged on until one morning the ugly duckling felt the sun warm on his back again.

He took off. His wings had grown and he could fly easily. He flew on until he was over a wide river. When he looked down there were some swans gliding along on the water.

'Come and join us,' called the swans.

'Oh, you don't want to swim with me! I'm only an ugly duckling,' he called back.

'A duckling?' laughed one of the swans.

'Come down and look at yourself. You're a swan just like us.'

The ugly duckling swooped down on to the river and gazed at his reflection in the water. And what he saw was not an ugly little grey duckling, but a beautiful white swan – just like the others. The other swans gathered around him. He was happy at last as they all flew off together.

How the Night Sky Became Brighter

Now this story happened many years ago, when the world was new. In the day the sky was blue and at night the sky was black. There were no stars and no moon to lighten the darkness. They had not yet been thought about. Early one morning two children called Mina and Lina made their way down to the river. They were chatting about this and that when suddenly - splash! — a blue slice of the sky fell down. And then a little further away — splash!

And then again – splash!
– and again – splash!

Mina and Lina looked up
into the sky and they could
see enormous holes in the blue.

The sky was falling so fast that
soon there was no more blue left at all – just
dark, rolling clouds.

The children turned and ran as fast as they
could back to the village.

'We must ask the hen wife what to do,' said
Mina. Now the hen wife was the wise
woman of the village. They ran
straight to her cottage.

The hen wife was
sitting outside her cottage,
shelling peas. She looked
at Mina and Lina, who
were puffing and panting
from all their running.

'You must gather all the pieces of sky that have fallen down and bring them to me. Then I will mend the sky.'

So off ran Mina and Lina to find all the pieces of sky. They took two large sacks and began to search.

There was sky everywhere. Some pieces had fallen into the stream, one piece was on the roof of a house, another piece had fallen on the apple tree in old Joseph's garden.

The children filled the sacks and took the pieces of sky back to the hen wife.

'Oh dear,' said the hen wife. 'There are not enough pieces here to fill all the gaps in the sky. Go and find something else to fill the spaces.'

Old Joseph wandered by. He sucked in his cheeks and said, 'The sky needs more than two colours. In the day it is blue and at night it is black. You must find other colours to brighten the sky.'

He whistled through his teeth, not once, but twice. Mina and Lina went back to the river, wondering what they could use to fill the spaces in the sky.

By the river they found some shiny coloured pebbles – red, blue, yellow, orange, green, golden, silver and purple.

They collected the pebbles and ran back to the hen wife.

We found these pebbles, but they are all different colours. We want the sky to be blue, as it has always been,' they said. 'It will look like a speckled egg if you put the coloured pebbles up there.'

The hen wife smiled at them and sent them to bed. Early the next morning Lina and Mina raced outside. The sky was blue again!

'How did you do it?' they asked the hen wife. But she just smiled. Old Joseph sucked in his cheeks and muttered as he took his ladder home. Lina saw that the blue tablecloth had a hole in it.

That night it was so hot that no-one could sleep. Lina and Mina tossed and turned.

In the end they went outside for some cool night air. They could smell the scent of the roses. 'Quick, quick,' shouted the girls. 'Come and see!' Soon all the villagers were awake. The dogs were barking and the cats stared up at the sky. It was no longer black. Each gap in the sky had been filled with a shiny pebble. They were glistening like a thousand fireflies in the darkness. The hen wife smiled. Old Joseph sucked in his cheeks. And Mina and Lina noticed that even his old eyes were as bright as the stars that night.